The Valentine Cat

The Valentine Cat

by

Ann Whitehead Nagda

illustrated by

Stephanie Roth

HOLIDAY HOUSE / *New York*

Text copyright © 2008 by Ann Whitehead Nagda
Illustrations copyright © 2008 by Stephanie Roth
All Rights Reserved
Printed in the United States of America
www.holidayhouse.com
First Edition
1   3   5   7   9   10   8   6   4   2

Library of Congress Cataloging-in-Publication Data

Nagda, Ann Whitehead, 1945-
The Valentine cat / by Ann Whitehead Nagda ; illustrated by Stephanie Roth.—1st ed.
p. cm.
Summary: Jenny writes an editorial for her fourth-grade classroom newspaper urging
that her beloved cat, Munchkin, become the official school cat, despite his mischievous
behavior before and during a Valentine's Day pet party.
ISBN 978-0-8234-2123-7 (hardcover)
[1. Cats—Fiction.   2. Schools—Fiction.   3. Journalism—Fiction.
4. Valentine's Day—Fiction.]   I. Roth, Stephanie, ill.   II. Title.
PZ7.N13355Val 2008
[Fic] —dc22
2008004224

To Sooty, the school cat at Llewellyn
Elementary School, and all the students
and staff who love him
—A. W. N.

To Ms. Sandy George,
Riverside Central
Elementary Librarian
—S. R.

Chapter 1

Jenny was going to be late to school. Her cat, Munchkin, escaped from her bedroom when she went to say good-bye. Just good-bye until after school, not good-bye forever. Not yet anyway.

Her cat could be so sneaky. He must have heard her footsteps in the hall. When she opened the door, he shot out of the room like a furry gray rocket.

Munchkin raced into her brother's room. Jenny spotted him under Toby's crib, hunched against the wall. She knelt down and talked to him softly. "You're not allowed in Toby's room anymore. Come on out like a good kitty."

The cat just stared at her with his big green eyes. Her mother had called him a cute little munchkin when he was a kitten. He was still cute, but he certainly wasn't little anymore. He started licking the gray fur on his paw.

"This is no time to take a bath," Jenny told him. When she tried to pull him out from under the crib, he hissed at her.

Finally Munchkin darted into her parents' bedroom. That's where her mother caught the fleeing cat. She folded him into her arms. "Oh, Munchkin, what are we going to do with you?" Her mother sighed before turning to Jenny. "The cat isn't happy stuck in your bedroom all day. If you can't find a friend to take him, I'll try some of my friends."

Jenny ran downstairs, blinking back tears. Sometimes life was so unfair.

Her father drove her to school. He tried to make conversation, but Jenny didn't want to talk. All she could think about was losing her cat.

The sidewalks and the playground were empty when they pulled up in front of the school. Jenny hurried inside and down the hall to her classroom. She threw her backpack and her coat into her cubby and slipped into her seat. Some of her class-mates were still wandering around the room. Maybe nobody had noticed that she was late.

Mary was showing Susan a book, and they were both squealing with delight. Jenny leaned toward Susan's desk. The book had pictures of little dogs wearing dresses. Jenny felt sorry for the dogs. If she were a dog, she didn't think she'd like wearing a dress. She didn't particularly like wearing dresses herself.

Mrs. Steele was writing some words on the board. Their teacher was wearing her ski outfit. She wore a blue sweater with white trees and snowflakes on it and dark wool pants.

Jenny wished she'd worn a heavy sweater, too. She looked outside. Flakes of snow were swirling through the air. She shivered and thought about her cat again. He was probably curled up on her bed.

"Today we're going to learn about writing a

newspaper article," said Mrs. Steele. "We're going to use the five Ws." She pointed to the board and read, "*Who? What? Where? When? Why?* How would we answer each of these questions if we were writing about our class pet?" She turned and gestured toward the tarantula's cage. "Let's start with *Who.*" She raised her eyebrows and looked at the class.

Lots of hands went up, but Kevin and Richard chorused, "Ruby."

Mrs. Steele wrote, "Ruby," next to "*Who*" on the blackboard.

"And how about the next question?" Their teacher pointed to *What.*

Susan's hand shot up. "*What* would explain more about Ruby. She's a Chilean rose tarantula and also our class pet."

Mrs. Steele wrote down everything Susan said.

Jenny took notes on the back of one of her math papers. Next to "*Who,*" she wrote, "*Susan.*" Next to "*What,*" she wrote, "*Class smarty-pants.*"

Mrs. Steele pointed to *Where.*

Mary said, "Our classroom."

"Or you could say, 'Mrs. Steele's fourth-grade classroom.'" Their teacher pointed to the board again. "Now *When* is a bit tricky. It could be *when* we first got the tarantula or *when* the tarantula did something exciting."

"Like when Ruby catches a cricket and eats it," said Richard.

"That's real exciting," muttered Kevin.

If *who* was *Kevin*, Jenny thought, then *what* would be *trouble*.

"*Why* could explain that tarantulas, like Ruby, eat crickets and other insects," said Susan.

"Or *why* we got a tarantula as a class pet," said Mary.

When Susan said something, Mary said something, too. Jenny wasn't sure *why*. Maybe Mary wanted to be just like Susan, perfect in every way.

"That's right. So *When* and *Why* sort of work together, don't they?" said their teacher. "Now I want you to write a paragraph using the five Ws. It can be about your own pet or our class pet."

Jenny frowned. She didn't want to write an article. Especially not about her pet. She raised her hand. "Do we have to share our paragraph?"

"Not if you don't want to," said Mrs. Steele.

Jenny was glad, because she didn't want to share her writing.

"During the next two weeks, we'll be working

on writing different kinds of articles," Mrs. Steele continued.

Kevin groaned. "You mean we have to write more than one article?"

Mrs. Steele nodded. "Yes, you will all write several articles. Then each student will select his or her best article, which will be printed in our classroom newspaper. Right now I'm just planning to publish our classroom newspaper once."

Jenny chewed on her pencil. She was not very good at writing things. Maybe she could write about Ruby. That wouldn't make her sad. But all she could think about was her cat.

Jenny wrote slowly. "My cat, Munchkin, lives at my house." That's *Who*, *What*, and *Where* in one short sentence. *When* was right now, so Jenny started her next sentence that way. "Right now she has to stay in my room." Four out of five. One more to go. The hard one was *Why*. She'd been asking herself that for days. *Why* did her brother have to get asthma? *Why* did the doctor say the cat had to go? *Why* couldn't they give away her brother instead? *Why* was complicated. *Why* was heartbreaking. She blinked hard, then caught a tear with her finger before it rolled down her face. She wrote quickly. "My brother has asthma, so we can't have a cat in the house. I have to give my cat away very soon, but I don't want to."

Mrs. Steele leaned over and touched her shoulder. "I'm so sorry," she whispered.

Jenny couldn't look at her teacher. Out of the corner of her eye, she could see nosy Susan watching. Jenny looked down at her desk.

"It's time for recess now," said Mrs. Steele. "When you come back inside, we'll share some of our writing."

Jenny was glad to get outside. Richard walked beside her. "You look sad," he said.

"I have to find a new home for my cat." She could feel a lump in her throat. She took a deep breath. "My brother has asthma."

"Maybe he could live at my house," said Richard.

"My brother?" asked Jenny.

"No, your cat."

"I'm not sure Munchkin would like your dog," said Jenny.

"My dog is pretty friendly," said Richard. "I'll ask my mom. If Munchkin lived at my house, you could see him every day."

That was true. But what if her cat forgot about her and liked Richard better? Jenny wanted Munchkin to be her very own cat forever.

Chapter 2

After recess Mrs. Steele asked for students to share their writing. Jenny was surprised when Richard volunteered to read first.

"My dog, Wolf, is older than I am. He is twelve years old. He helped raise me. Wolf has a doghouse in the backyard, but he'd rather sleep on the dirty clothes in my room. He likes my smell."

Jenny smiled at him. She liked Richard a lot.

"Nice, Richard," said Mrs. Steele. "Who else would like to share?"

Kevin marched to the front of the room. "Ruby is the pet tarantula in Mrs. Steele's room." He paused. "That's *Who, What,* and *Where.*"

Mrs. Steele nodded. "Good, Kevin. Do you have more?"

"Yes," said Kevin. "Here's *When.*" He looked

down at his paper. His mouth moved, but no words came out.

Jenny stared at him and tried to read his lips. Maybe he'd lost his place. Maybe he couldn't read his messy handwriting. She wished someone would help him.

Finally Kevin pointed to the middle of his paper. "Okay, I've found it. When Ruby eats a cricket, she squirts some stuff on it. The stuff turns it into cricket juice. She does that because she has to drink her food. She can't chomp it like people do."

Everyone laughed.

"Who else would like to read?" asked Mrs. Steele.

Susan pranced to the front of the room. She waited until everyone was quiet. "This is an article about something fun we could do in two weeks." She pawed the floor with a bright red shoe that matched her red sweater and red rosebud earrings. "I wrote it like we're really going to do it."

When Susan had a good idea, she usually made it happen. Not that Jenny was jealous. It was just that one person shouldn't have all the good ideas all the time.

Susan cleared her throat and started to read. "Mrs. Steele's fourth-grade class is doing something unusual for Valentine's Day this year. They are going to have a pet party. Each student will bring a pet to class dressed up in a costume. They will celebrate their pets and share them with the class as well."

"That sounds like fun," said Mrs. Steele. "Raise your hand if you'd like to have a pet party."

Jenny sighed. A pet party would be fun if you had a pet.

Lots of hands went up.

Mrs. Steele looked around the room. "It's almost unanimous," she said. "We'll start planning the pet party."

Jenny started to plan being absent on Valentine's Day.

"Mary brought a book to school today," Susan said. "It has pictures of dogs wearing costumes. Would it be okay if she showed it to the class?"

"That would be fun." Mrs. Steele motioned for Mary to come up to the front of the room.

Mary stood beside Susan and held up the book. "This dog is wearing a clown costume." She turned to another page. "Here's a dog wearing a crocodile suit. And look at this picture. A poodle is dressed as a bumblebee."

"Show us the picture of the Chihuahua in the princess dress," said Susan.

Mary fumbled with the book. Finally she found the right page and held it up.

"Doesn't that dog look adorable!" said Susan.

Jenny thought the dog did look cute.

She heard Richard snort, so she turned around to look at him. He was grinning. "I can't wait to put a tutu on our tarantula," he whispered. "Won't she look adorable?"

Richard always made her smile. Even when she felt sad.

"Do we have to make a costume?" Rana asked.

"You don't have to," said Susan. "A special collar or a colorful hat would be nice. Here is a Chihuahua with pearls around her neck." Susan took the book from Mary and held up a picture.

"Someone just took a pearl necklace and wound it around the dog's neck a few times," Mary added.

Jenny put her head down on her desk. She wouldn't have a pet for the Valentine's Day party. And she had to write lots of articles in the next two weeks. How much worse could things get?

Chapter 3

Richard called after dinner. "My mother says you can bring the cat over anytime. Do you want to bring him tonight?"

Jenny didn't want to bring him at all, but definitely not right away. She started to get a lump in her throat. The kind you get when you try not to cry.

"Hello. Are you still there?" Richard asked.

Jenny swallowed. It was hard to talk. "Tomorrow," she finally said. Tomorrow was Saturday, and she'd have the weekend to get used to not having a cat anymore.

Jenny went into the living room. Her mother was sitting on the couch while her brother played on the floor with his dump truck.

"Vroom. Vroom." Toby was making engine noises as he crawled around with the truck. He was two years old and a lot of trouble.

"Richard's family is going to take Munchkin tomorrow," she told her mom.

"I know it's hard on you, honey," her mother said, "but I'm glad that your friend's family is willing to take care of our cat."

"Play with kitty," said her brother, Toby.

"You can't play with the kitty," said her mother. "The kitty will make you sick."

"Play with kitty," Toby said louder.

"Jenny, could you find Toby's bear? Maybe that will get his mind off the . . ." Her mother paused, then spelled out, "C-a-t."

Jenny sighed. She was in no mood to play "find the bear" for her brother. She didn't mind if he cried about the cat. He should cry about it, the little pest. But then he started to wail. Quickly Jenny peered under the couch. No bear. She crawled across the floor and looked behind the big blue chair. There it was. She picked up the small, fuzzy bear and tossed it at her brother. Bull's-eye. It hit him in the chest.

Her mother gave her a stern look.

Fortunately, Toby didn't mind getting bonked by a flying bear. He put the bear in his truck and took it for a ride around the coffee table.

"I'll pack up the cat's food and toys after I put

Toby to bed," said her mom. "We can take Munchkin to Richard's house first thing in the morning."

Jenny nodded, then hurried upstairs. She had only one more night with her cat. She didn't want to waste any of it.

Munchkin was curled on her bed with all four paws together. Jenny lay on the bed beside him and rubbed his ears. He started to purr. A tear rolled down Jenny's face.

She got up, wiped her eyes, and put on her pajamas. After she brushed her teeth, she picked up a book and sat on her bed with her back propped up with a pillow. She tried to read, but then she'd look at Munchkin.

"I'm going to miss you," she said. Another tear rolled down her face.

The cat raised his head and stared at Jenny. He stood up and touched her arm with his paw. Jenny scrunched down so that only her head was on the pillow and pulled Munchkin closer. He sat down on her chest and purred so hard that she could feel the vibration deep inside her body. That made her cry even more. Finally she fell asleep, but woke up many times during the night. She knew her cat was close by because she could hear his little snorts and wheezes. Her brother made sounds like that, too, but his asthma wheezes were scary.

By the time Jenny stumbled down to breakfast, her mother had everything but the cat packed into the car. The cat didn't want to go into his yellow cat carrier at first. He spread his legs so that he wouldn't fit through the door. Jenny's mother tossed a cat treat into the carrier, and Munchkin trotted after it. Her father had taken Toby to the family room so that he wouldn't see the cat leaving and start to fuss.

Once in the car, Jenny sat in the backseat next to the cat. She stuck a finger through the bars of the carrier door. Munchkin licked her finger. Then he meowed.

"Poor kitty, you don't know what's happening, do you?" said Jenny's mom.

The cat meowed again. It sounded even sadder than his first meow. Jenny was sure Munchkin knew something bad was happening.

When they arrived at Richard's house, he came outside to help carry the kitty supplies.

"We put the dog in the basement so he won't scare the cat." Richard grabbed the bag of cat food.

Jenny's mom picked up the cat carrier while Jenny carried the litter box into the house. Richard

led the way to a bedroom. "This is going to be Munchkin's room."

Jenny looked around the room. It had a bed and a dresser but was otherwise pretty empty. She hoped her cat wouldn't have to spend too much time there. She took a few of Munchkin's toys out of a box while her mom poured cat food into his bowl and Richard went to get some water.

"We got instructions from the Humane Society about introducing a cat and dog," explained Richard's mom. "First they need to get used to each other's scent. Then tomorrow we'll let them see each other for thirty seconds at a time while the dog is on a leash."

Jenny opened the door to the carrier. Munchkin didn't come out. Jenny peered inside. "Come on," she coaxed.

Richard sat down next to Jenny.

Munchkin finally came out and sniffed Richard. Then the cat ran under the bed.

"Do I smell that bad?" Richard said. "I'm positive my shirt was washed last month."

Jenny ignored him and lay on the floor peering under the bed.

"We'll let the cat get used to this room first," said Richard's mom, "then let him explore the rest

of the house when the dog isn't around, either today or tomorrow."

Jenny's mother said, "That sounds like a good idea." She looked at her watch. "I need to go now and get Toby ready for a doctor's appointment."

Toby went to the doctor a lot. Sometimes Jenny felt sorry for him, but not today. She looked at her scared cat and decided she couldn't leave him. "I think I'd better stay with Munchkin for a while," she said.

Richard's mother brought Jenny some magazines to read.

"I'll go and take the dog for a walk." Richard stood up. "Maybe the cat will come out if I'm not here."

Jenny nodded and picked up a magazine. After a few minutes the cat crawled out and sat down beside her. She pulled him onto her lap. "Poor kitty."

Richard knocked on the door after she had looked at three magazines. He held out a Monopoly game. "Would you like to play?"

"Sure," said Jenny.

When they were an hour into the game, Munchkin reached out and pushed Jenny's hotel off the board.

"I think the cat is feeling better," said Jenny.

"Maybe he's trying to help me beat you." Richard grinned.

After the game, Jenny and Richard ate sandwiches while watching a movie in the family room.

Munchkin sat next to Jenny on the couch. She gave him a tiny piece of turkey, which he licked from her hand. Then with claws extended on one paw, the cat tried to snag more meat from her sandwich.

"No, no!" Jenny held her plate away.

The cat stood on her lap and reached toward the sandwich.

Jenny pushed him off her lap and stood to finish her lunch.

"Munchkin has great table manners," said Richard. "Do you often stand to eat at your house?"

Jenny finished her last bite of sandwich. "I shouldn't have fed the cat from my lunch, but I felt sorry for him."

It was late afternoon when Jenny's mother came to pick her up. Jenny carried her cat back to the bedroom, put on her coat, and said good-bye. Munchkin meowed when she closed the door. To Jenny it sounded like a very sad meow.

Chapter 4

Jenny was at school early on Monday morning hoping to talk to Richard, but he was late. She had called him several times over the weekend to ask about the cat. He always said the cat was fine.

"How is Munchkin today?" Jenny asked him as soon as he was seated.

"Okay," said Richard.

"I want to know exactly what Munchkin is doing. Is he eating?"

"I'm not sure," said Richard.

"What do you mean, you're not sure?" asked Jenny.

"Well, last night my mom brought Munchkin into the family room to watch TV with us," said Richard. "He sat on my mom's lap."

"Did he purr?"

"No, but I think he liked the show. It looked like he was watching it. Anyway, we thought Wolf was locked in the basement. But he got into the cat's room and ate all the food."

"All the food in the big bag?" Jenny imagined Wolf with a bulging stomach.

"No, just the food from the cat's bowl," said Richard. "That's why we don't know if the cat ate anything."

"What happened when Wolf met Munchkin?" asked Jenny.

"Well." Richard hesitated. "Wolf wagged his tail."

Jenny had a bad feeling. There was something Richard didn't want to tell her. "But what did Munchkin do?"

Richard chewed on his lower lip. Finally he said, "Your cat is very good at hissing."

"So he doesn't like your dog?" Jenny asked.

Richard shrugged his shoulders. "Not unless spitting and growling means 'I like you' in cat language."

"Purring means 'I like you,'" said Jenny.

"We haven't heard any purring," said Richard.

Susan had been listening to their conversation. "Is Jenny's cat living at your house now?" she asked.

"Yes," said Richard, "but he spends a lot of time hiding under the dresser."

"That's not good," said Susan. "I don't think dogs and cats get along very well."

"The Humane Society says they can be trained to be together," said Richard. "Although it can take a while."

"How long is a while?" Jenny asked.

"Several months," said Richard.

Now Jenny was really worried about her cat. Munchkin might be unhappy for months and months.

Mrs. Steele stood in front of the room. She was wearing a green sweater with little dogs on it. The dogs on the sweater looked like cute little dogs. Maybe cats could be trained to like cute little dogs, but not big scary dogs like Wolf.

"Today we're going to talk about leads," their teacher said. "The lead is the beginning of an article. It needs to hook the reader."

"Like a fishhook?" asked Richard.

"Yes. A fishhook helps a fisherman catch a fish," agreed Mrs. Steele, "and you want your lead to catch the reader's attention. Take out the pet article you wrote last week."

Jenny found her article right away, but she could hear Richard rummaging through his desk. She turned around.

"I can't find my article." Richard held out a handful of papers, some folded, some torn.

Jenny felt sorry for him. He might have to write his article all over again.

"What interesting fact could you use to begin your article?" asked Mrs. Steele.

Susan raised her hand. "Mrs. Steele's fourth-grade class is having a new kind of party for Valentine's Day. That's the lead, and then my article explains the pet party idea."

"Yes, Susan, that would be a good way to start your article," said their teacher. "Another way to start an article is with a question. Can someone give me an example of a question lead?"

Susan's hand shot up again.

Their teacher looked around the room, but nobody else's hand was up. She nodded at Susan.

"Are you tired of having the same kind of party every Valentine's Day?"

"Good," said Mrs. Steele. "Anyone else? Some of you wrote about Ruby, our tarantula. Can you think of an interesting fact or a question that would make someone want to read your article?"

Rana raised her hand. "Can you imagine eating something that's half as big as you are?"

"That's a great lead," said Mrs. Steele. "Any other ideas?"

"Can you imagine eating a cricket for lunch?" Kevin made gagging noises.

"That question would get someone's attention, wouldn't it?" Mrs. Steele wrinkled her nose. "Now we're going to talk about the three parts of an article. The lead is the first part. Next comes the body, where you answer the five Ws. And last is the conclusion. Think about how you want to end your article. You can end your story with something the reader could think about or you can propose a solution to something."

Kevin groaned. "Do we have to write our stupid article again?"

"Yes," said Mrs. Steele. "But I want you to work with a partner so that you can help each other. Work with the person next to you."

Jenny felt like groaning, too. She had to work with Susan.

Richard's desk was rattling as he searched it again. Jenny turned to look at him.

"Saved," he muttered as he pulled out a crumpled piece of paper.

Rana laughed and moved her chair next to Richard's desk.

Jenny wished she could work with Richard. She moved her chair closer to Susan's desk.

"Let me see your article," said Susan.

Jenny passed it to her.

Susan read the article quickly, then stared at the paper with a serious look on her face.

Jenny worried that Susan didn't like her article.

Finally Susan turned to her and said, "This is very sad. It must be hard to lose your cat."

Susan was being so nice that Jenny was afraid she'd cry.

"I'm trying to think of a good lead for your article." Susan was back to being all business. "How old is your cat?"

"Munchkin is five. My parents got him as a kitten." Jenny wasn't sure how Susan could make a lead out of that.

Susan had started writing on her paper. "How would you like to lose a pet that's lived with you for five years?" She looked at Jenny. "Do you like that lead? Or we can start with a fact instead." She wrote something else on the paper. "Munchkin, a friendly male cat, has to leave the only home he's ever known."

Jenny was amazed that Susan could come up with things so quickly. Of course, she was the best writer in the class.

"Which lead do you like better?" asked Susan.

"I like the second lead, the one with the fact," said Jenny.

"The new lead explains *Who* and *What*," Susan continued. "Now we need to know *Where*. So you could write, 'He has lived with the Millers for five years.'"

"Okay." Jenny wrote that down.

"For the next sentence you can say, 'Their son, Toby, has asthma. The cat makes him sick.'"

"You left out *When*," Jenny pointed out. She was glad to be able to correct Susan about something.

Susan wrote the word *now* after *asthma*.

"Their son, Toby, has asthma now," Jenny read.

Susan said, "Now you need a good ending."

They certainly did. But Jenny didn't know what a good ending would be.

"Hmmm." Susan looked at the ceiling.

Jenny looked up, too, but she didn't see anything helpful. She chewed on her pencil.

"How about, 'Once they find a new home for the cat, everyone will feel better'?" Susan smiled triumphantly.

"I guess that's okay." Jenny tried not to frown. "But I won't feel better unless Munchkin is happy, too. And he doesn't sound very happy at Richard's house."

"Maybe Munchkin can live at my house," said Susan. "Of course, I'll have to ask my mother first."

Jenny wondered if her cat would like perfect Susan and her perfect house. On the other hand, she was desperate to find a good home for her pet. She suddenly thought of a good reason for her cat to move in with Susan. "If Munchkin lives with you, he can come to the pet party with your cat."

"That's right," Susan said. "I've been thinking about making a gorgeous pink dress for Portia to wear to the pet party. She'll be a cat princess. What about a tiara! My kitty would look fabulous wearing a tiara with her gown." Susan was so excited her eyes were shining. "Munchkin can be the cat prince and wear a purple suit. Won't they look darling together?"

Jenny nodded. She tried to picture Munchkin in a purple suit sitting next to Susan's cat and looking darling. If Munchkin really liked Portia, it might work.

During recess, Susan called her mother.

Jenny stood nearby, hardly daring to hope that Susan's mother would agree. She tried to picture her cat in Susan's house. The living room had big windows that looked out over the backyard. On nice days Munchkin would be able to stretch out in the sunlight and snooze. He'd like that. There were several bird feeders in the yard, too. Munchkin liked watching birds.

Susan closed her phone and gave Jenny a

thumbs-up. "Bring Munchkin over this afternoon, and we can introduce him to Portia."

Jenny was relieved. "That's great," she told Susan. At least Jenny hoped the meeting of the two cats would be great. And her cat wouldn't have to live at Richard's house anymore. If everything went well, Munchkin would like Portia and Susan and her house and her mother. But that was a lot for a cat to like all at once.

Chapter 5

After school Jenny's mother drove her to Richard's house to pick up the cat.

When Richard answered the door, he didn't look happy. "Munchkin has been hiding under the bed all day and won't come out."

"Where's Wolf?" Jenny asked.

"I put him in the basement," said Richard. "He was sitting outside the cat's room when I got home, wagging his tail."

"Wolf seems to like the cat," said Richard's mom. "He sits outside that door a lot, waiting to make friends."

Jenny followed Richard upstairs.

As soon as Jenny entered the room, she knelt on the floor and looked under the bed. Two eyes gleamed in the darkness. "Poor kitty," Jenny said.

Munchkin crawled out when he heard Jenny's voice. She rubbed his ears, and he climbed into her lap.

Richard sat down beside her. "He doesn't seem to be eating either."

"We talked to our vet today," said Richard's mother. "He said that some cats never feel comfortable around a dog."

Jenny leaned over and kissed the cat's head. "What if Munchkin doesn't like Susan's cat?"

Richard patted the cat. "Anything would be better than spending the day under a bed."

Jenny had to agree with that.

"Let's just take Munchkin to Susan's house right now," said Jenny's mom. "We can come back later and get the rest of his food and his litter box."

"Good idea," said Richard's mother. "If it doesn't work out at Susan's, you can always bring the cat back here, and we'll keep trying to make him feel at home."

Jenny hoped that wouldn't be necessary.

Munchkin didn't put up any fuss about going into his carrier.

When they arrived at Susan's house, Jenny's mom picked up the cat carrier. "You're going to love it here," her mother told the cat. She tried to

smile at Jenny, but it looked more like a frown. "I'm trying to be positive about this."

Jenny had a sinking feeling. Her mom probably wasn't counting on a successful cat meeting either.

Susan's mother opened the door. "Come in, come in. Susan has Portia upstairs." She led them to the kitchen, then leaned over and looked in the door of Munchkin's carrier. "How are you?" she said to the cat. She stood up. "What a lovely cat. Why don't you open the door to his carrier and let him come out and look around?"

Jenny's mother set the carrier on the floor. Jenny opened the door and spoke softly to her cat. "Don't be scared." As the cat came out she touched his back and whispered, "Be a nice kitty."

And Munchkin was nice at first. He rubbed his head on Jenny's shoe. He smelled Susan's mother's feet. He sniffed the floor by the pantry. He sniffed under the kitchen table. Then he jumped onto the gleaming kitchen counter.

Susan's mother gasped.

Obviously, she wasn't used to a curious cat. Jenny held her breath.

Her mother snatched the cat off the counter. "What a spacious kitchen. And the backyard is gorgeous."

Susan's mother smiled. "My husband loves to work in the garden." She led them into the living room and motioned toward a flowered sofa. "Please, sit down."

Jenny sat next to her mother. Munchkin wouldn't sit down. He stood on her mother's lap and looked around the room. He sprang to the floor and headed for a planter box on the floor by the window. The box was smaller than her brother's sandbox but large enough to be a cat play area. At first Munchkin sniffed the leaves hanging over the side of the box. But then he couldn't resist. The cat jumped into the box and crouched down like he was hiding in a jungle.

Susan's mother moaned. "My lovely plants!"

"I don't have any live plants in our house," Jenny's mother explained. "I guess the cat isn't used to plants."

"He's very curious." Jenny stood up, but before she could reach the cat, he started to dig.

Susan's mother hurried over and whipped the cat out of the planter. "No, no, no!" she told the cat as she handed him to Jenny. "Hold the cat while I get a cloth to clean his muddy paws."

Jenny sat down in a chair and snuggled the cat against her stomach, holding him tight. She knew Munchkin didn't like having his paws touched.

Susan's mom rushed back with a wet washcloth.

Jenny was glad her cat only struggled a little while his paws were being washed. "It's okay," she told him softly.

"Shall I bring Portia downstairs?" Susan asked.

"Maybe you should wait until Munchkin has finished licking his paws," said Jenny. "Then I'll comb him because that always makes him happy."

Munchkin sat on Jenny's lap and carefully washed each one of his four paws with his tongue. As soon as he stopped washing, Jenny pulled a comb from her pocket and ran it over his back. He started to purr. "That's a good kitty," she whispered. "Keep on purring."

But as soon as Susan appeared with her cat, Munchkin reacted. His purring stopped and his tail puffed up.

Susan set Portia down on the carpet, unaware that Munchkin was not acting the least bit friendly.

Munchkin dug his claws into Jenny's legs, which made her let go of him. The cat sprang off Jenny's lap and charged at Portia, hissing and spitting.

Susan grabbed her cat and ran upstairs.

Munchkin shook himself and stopped hissing. He turned and trotted back to Jenny, acting like he was proud of himself for chasing away the intruder. Then he sat down and began to wash his paws again.

Susan's mother sighed. "I'm afraid they're not going to get along."

If she was trying to look disappointed, she failed.

Jenny stood up and went to the kitchen to get the cat carrier. So much for Prince Munchkin and Princess Portia.

As her mother drove back to Richard's house, she said, "Susan's house was so neat and clean. I didn't notice a speck of dust anywhere."

"Munchkin needs a home that isn't so perfect," said Jenny.

Her mother nodded in agreement. "He needs a nice, messy house without another cat or dog."

"All my friends have either cats or dogs," Jenny said sadly.

"Maybe we'll have to advertise in the paper," said her mother.

"I don't want a stranger to take Munchkin!" Jenny shouted. "That would be awful."

Her mother stopped at a stoplight and looked at her with sad eyes. "Then I guess he'll just have to stay with Richard until we come up with something better."

Jenny didn't know what else to do.

Chapter 6

On Wednesday morning Mrs. Steele was wearing her safari outfit: tan pants, a leopard-print sweater, and matching leopard-print shoes.

"Today we're going to talk about interviewing people. If you were writing for a school newspaper, you might interview one of the teachers at the school or you might interview a student who is doing something special. Before the interview, make a list of questions. During the interview, you may use a tape recorder, but you should also take notes."

"What if we don't have a tape recorder?" asked Kevin.

"Then just take notes," said Mrs. Steele. "Now I want you all to pretend that you are reporters. You are going to interview me. Think of some questions you would like to ask."

Kevin guffawed.

Mrs. Steele looked at him sternly. "Be serious about this. Write a few questions on a piece of paper."

Jenny pulled a piece of paper from her desk and stared at it. "Did you have any pets when you were a child?" she wrote. Pets were all she could think about. "Do you have any pets now?" If her teacher didn't have a pet, maybe she'd like a cat. A scared cat named Munchkin, who was probably hiding under the bed at Richard's house.

Richard leaned over her shoulder and read her questions. He chuckled.

Jenny looked at him, and he smiled. What was he smiling about? Her questions weren't funny.

Mrs. Steele pulled her desk chair to the front of the room and sat down. "I'm ready to be interviewed," she said.

"Do we have to take notes now?" Kevin asked.

"No, you don't," said Mrs. Steele. "This is just a practice interview."

Susan raised her hand. "How long have you been a teacher?"

"I've been teaching for eight years," said Mrs. Steele.

"Have you always taught fourth grade?" Susan continued.

"No," said their teacher, "I taught third grade first."

"Which grade do you like best?" Susan asked.

Jenny wondered if Susan would ask all the questions and nobody else would get to say anything.

"I like fourth grade best." Mrs. Steele smiled. "Now let's give someone else a chance to ask something."

Rana raised her hand. "Where did you grow up?"

"I grew up in Chicago," said Mrs. Steele.

"Did you ever get in trouble when you were little?" Kevin asked with a sly grin.

"I got lost one time at the zoo," said their teacher.

"Were you scared?" asked Rana.

"A nice family stayed with me until my father found me," said Mrs. Steele.

"Did you have any pets?" asked Jenny. There, she got to ask her question before someone else did.

"Yes, I had a parakeet and a hamster."

"Do you have any pets now?" Richard's voice boomed in Jenny's ear.

Hey, that was Jenny's next question. She turned around to look at Richard, and he winked.

"No, I don't."

Richard raised his eyebrows and grinned. "How would you like a pet cat?"

Jenny grinned back. She didn't have the nerve to ask that question.

"I'm not home very much," said Mrs. Steele, "so I'm afraid a cat would get lonely."

"You could bring him to school," said Richard.

"Maybe I could." Mrs. Steele laughed. "Whose cat are we talking about?" She looked at Jenny.

Jenny could feel herself turning red. Oh, wouldn't it be wonderful if her teacher would adopt her cat? She knew Munchkin would be happy with Mrs. Steele.

"Jenny's cat is living at my house right now," Richard explained, "but he doesn't like my dog."

Mrs. Steele looked at Jenny again. "Would you like to have your cat spend a week or two in our classroom?"

Jenny nodded. She would love to have her cat in the classroom. She was afraid it was too wonderful to be true.

"Does anyone have cat allergies?" asked the teacher.

Jenny held her breath. She looked around the room. No one raised a hand.

"Good," said Mrs. Steele. "I'll talk to the principal at lunchtime about a class cat."

Jenny smiled. A class cat would be so much better than a big old tarantula. She hoped the principal wouldn't mind having a cat at school. Maybe Munchkin would be able to stay in her classroom long enough to attend the pet party. Or maybe Mrs. Steele would love Munchkin so much that she would adopt him and bring him to class with her every day. If only it could work out!

Chapter 7

Mrs. Perry, the principal, liked the idea of a visiting cat but added that Munchkin must behave and not disrupt classroom lessons or cause problems for kids with allergies. So the next morning Jenny and her mother collected the cat, his food, litter, and all the rest of his stuff from Richard's house. Jenny sat in the backseat with the cat. Richard climbed into the front seat.

"You need to be very good today," Jenny told her cat. "And every day for the next two weeks."

Richard guffawed. "Fat chance," he said.

Jenny worried that he was right. Her kitty liked to get into things.

Munchkin meowed.

"I didn't feed the cat this morning," said Richard. "Not that he'd eat at my house anyway. Maybe if he eats breakfast in our classroom, he'll get the idea that it's his new home."

"Are you hungry, kitty?" asked Jenny.

The cat meowed again.

"Me-yessss." Richard imitated the cat's plaintive meow.

As soon as they got out of the car at school, several kids surrounded Richard, who held the cat carrier. "What's in there? Is the cat for show-and-tell?"

Jenny had been worried that kids would pester her cat. They weren't even inside the school yet and it had already started.

"Stand back," said Richard. "This is a ferocious beast."

"He doesn't look ferocious," said another kid.

"Say GRRRRRRR, kitty." Richard growled like an angry tiger.

Munchkin didn't say anything. Not a peep.

Jenny's mother unloaded a red wagon from the back of the car. She hoisted the bag of cat food into it.

"Why do you have all that food?" said a kid in a brown jacket.

"That's not for the cat," said Richard. "That's what the cafeteria is serving for lunch today."

Jenny couldn't help laughing. Richard's jokes always made her feel better.

When they got to the classroom, Mrs. Steele let the students following them peek at the cat from the doorway, but she wouldn't let them into the classroom if they weren't part of her fourth-grade class. "We don't want to scare the kitty on his first day at our school."

Mrs. Steele pointed out a spot in the back of the room where Richard could put the litter box. Jenny set the cat's bowls nearby and filled them. She sat on the floor and offered dried cat food to Munchkin. The cat ate the pellets from her hand, but didn't seem interested in eating from his bowl.

When the bell rang, Jenny picked her cat up and carried him to her desk.

"Would you like to introduce your cat to the class, Jenny?" Mrs. Steele stood beside Jenny and rubbed the cat behind his ears. "You're a lovely kitty, aren't you?" The cat closed his eyes and pushed his head against her hand.

Jenny really didn't like talking in front of the whole class. She held her cat close. "This is my cat, Munchkin," she said. "He's going to live in our classroom for a little while."

"He's adorable." Rana patted the cat's back.

Several other students gathered around the cat and touched him. Jenny was surprised that Munchkin didn't mind. In fact, he seemed to like all the attention.

"How old is he?" asked Rana.

"He's five," said Jenny.

"Just the right age to start school," said Richard.

Mrs. Steele walked to the front of the room. "Okay, class, everybody sit down and leave the cat alone for a while so that he can get used to our classroom."

Jenny sat down. Munchkin jumped out of her lap and sat down on the floor right beside her chair.

"Today we're going to work on interviews again," their teacher continued. "I want you to find a partner, and then you and your partner will interview each other. Find out some interesting things about your classmate. Then I want you to write an article about that person."

Jenny stood up.

Munchkin stood up, too.

Jenny pulled her chair next to Richard's desk. She didn't want to get stuck with Susan again.

Munchkin jumped onto Richard's desk and sat down.

"See, your cat likes me," said Richard. "I think he wants to be interviewed."

Jenny rolled her eyes.

Richard pulled out a blank piece of paper. "Munchkin, how do you like being at school?"

Richard answered in a high voice, pretending to be a cat. "School is great as long as no big dogs or cats come around." He scribbled some notes on the paper. "You can ask some questions, too."

"How did you like living at Richard's house?" Jenny asked.

"I never want to go back to that dump." Richard grinned.

Jenny giggled. "Your house isn't a dump, Richard."

Richard answered in the cat's voice. "It would feel like a dump if you spent all your time under a bed." He made some more notes on his paper. Then he switched to his interviewer's voice. "We're having a pet party next week. I'm afraid there will be several dogs and cats. What will you do during the party?"

Uh-oh, Jenny thought, that may be a problem.

"I'll hide out in the library," Richard said in his cat voice. "Nando will protect me."

"Have you met Nando, the librarian, yet?" Richard switched to his interviewer's voice.

"No, but Jenny told me he's a nice guy," said Richard in his cat voice.

Munchkin crossed his paws.

"See." Richard turned to Jenny. "Munchkin likes being interviewed." He addressed the cat again. "Are you planning to wear a costume for the Valentine's party?"

"I won't wear a purple tutu, that's for sure," Jenny answered for Munchkin.

Richard patted the cat. "I don't blame you. I

wouldn't wear a purple tutu either." He set his pen down.

With one paw the cat reached out and pushed the pen off the desk.

"Does that mean the interview is over?" asked Richard.

Munchkin stretched out and put his head down on the desk.

"I guess it does." Richard turned to Jenny. "Now you get to ask me some questions."

"Maybe I should interview the tarantula," said Jenny.

"Or the crickets." Richard pointed to the bookcase. "Look at them over there bouncing around."

The cat lifted his head and stared at the crickets, too.

"Mr. Cricket, how do you feel about being spider food?" asked Richard.

"What a way to go! Chirp! Chirp!" He pretended to be a cricket and spoke while holding his nose, which made his voice sound like he had a bad cold.

"Let me interview you," said Jenny. "You're more interesting than a cricket."

"Really? Oh, thank you, thank you." Richard gave her a big smile.

"Now you have to be serious," said Jenny. "Where were you born?"

"That's a very serious question," said Richard. "I was born in Colorado."

Jenny wrote that down. "Tell me about your brother."

"My brother gets into my stuff, which makes me mad." He made a face like an angry tiger.

"What kind of stuff does your brother get into?" Jenny asked.

"He takes my skateboard and leaves it outside in the bushes. He even raided my stocking on Christmas morning." Now Richard growled like a tiger.

"Did Santa bring you something nice?" Jenny asked.

"Who knows? All that was left in my stocking was an orange!"

Jenny agreed that little brothers could be a problem. She decided to ask about something else. "What do you like to do after school?"

"My homework. I adore homework," Richard said.

Now Jenny knew he was kidding. "What about on the weekend?"

"I like to watch sad kitties hide under the bed." Richard plunked his elbow down on the edge of the desk and rested his chin on his fist.

Munchkin raised his head and looked wide-eyed at Jenny.

"You scared the cat," Jenny told him.

Richard sat up straight and spoke in his high cat voice again. "You're such a dope, Richard."

Jenny laughed. She rubbed the cat under his chin, where his fur was supersoft. Munchkin lifted his head and closed his eyes with pleasure.

"Don't forget to switch, so both you and your partner get to do an interview," said Mrs. Steele.

"Then I want you to think of a good lead and write your article. We'll share them tomorrow."

"Okay," said Richard. "My turn to interview you."

Jenny wrinkled her nose. "You already interviewed my cat, so you don't need to interview me." She moved back to her own desk.

Munchkin stayed on Richard's desk.

Richard chuckled.

Jenny turned to look at him. He only had a little bit of desk to write on. Munchkin took up most of the desk. Richard was writing really fast.

Jenny rested her chin on the back of her hand and chewed on the end of her pencil. She tried to think of a lead for her article about Richard. She wrote, "Richard's Christmas stocking was empty except for an orange." No, she didn't like that lead. Maybe a question would be better. "What do you do when your brother raids your stuff?" But then all she could think of to write was that Richard was mad and growled.

Jenny's article was still only two sentences long when Mrs. Steele told them to line up for lunch.

Munchkin looked up as the class marched out the door, but then he put his head down again. Jenny made sure she was last in line so that she could close the classroom door tight.

After lunch Jenny wasn't surprised to find Munchkin sound asleep on her teacher's rocking chair, which had plump, soft cushions. At her house he'd always found the most comfortable spots for sleeping. When Mrs. Steele picked him up to use the chair herself, he hissed at her. Jenny rushed over and grabbed her naughty cat. "He doesn't hiss very often," she told her teacher.

Mrs. Steele said, "I guess I shouldn't have disturbed his nap," but she didn't smile and her voice sounded funny.

Jenny didn't know if her teacher was sad or mad or just surprised.

When the bell rang at the end of the day, Jenny put on her coat and hat. She worried about leaving her cat. "Will Munchkin be okay in the school all night long?" she asked her teacher.

"I'm sure he'll be fine. I'll shut the classroom door when I go home," said Mrs. Steele, "and ask the custodian to check on him."

"What about the weekend?" asked Jenny.

"Someone will take him home." Mrs. Steele smiled. "I'm still working on that."

Jenny hoped her teacher would take care of Munchkin. But maybe Mrs. Steele didn't like cats that hissed.

Chapter 8

The next morning Munchkin greeted Jenny when she entered the classroom. The cat rubbed against her legs and then headed toward the back of the room.

"Are you hungry?" Jenny asked. She looked at his food bowl, but there was plenty of food. Her teacher must have filled it when she got to school.

While Mrs. Steele counted the students who wanted hot lunch, Munchkin sat beside Jenny's chair. Soon, though, he got up and sniffed Susan's shoes and then Rana's.

"There are three types of newspaper stories," Mrs. Steele told the class. She went to the board and wrote, "Types of newspaper stories."

Jenny looked around the room for Munchkin. Oh, no, he was on the top of the bookcase watching the crickets jump around. His nose was pressed against the plastic side of the cage. When the cat had jumped up there yesterday, Richard said Munchkin was watching "Kitty TV." He thought it would keep the cat amused and out of trouble. Jenny wasn't so sure.

Mrs. Steele said, "Hard news stories are about recent events." She wrote, "Hard News Stories," on the board.

Jenny looked at the board. She thought that all stories were hard to write. If there were easy news stories, she'd like to know about them.

"Why are they called hard news stories?" asked Mary.

"Hard news stories are just the facts about an event," said their teacher. "Human-interest stories are another kind of story about people and places. They're meant to be more entertaining than hard news, so they're called soft news. The articles about your classmates are soft news."

Jenny's story about Richard didn't seem very soft. It was just short.

Mrs. Steele wrote, "Human-interest Stories," on the board. "The third type of story is an editorial. That's where you can write an opinion about something." On the board she wrote, "Editorials."

Jenny looked at the board, then over at her cat. The only opinion she had at the moment was that her cat should be moved away from the crickets.

With one paw Munchkin nudged the plastic cage, moving it toward the edge of the shelf.

Jenny stood up. Before she could get to her cat, Munchkin pushed the cricket cage off the shelf. The cat peered over the side as the cage crashed to the floor. The lid popped off, and crickets sprang everywhere. The cat leaped down to the floor and sprang after one of them. Several kids screamed. Richard laughed as he leaped after another cricket.

This was no laughing matter for Jenny. Her naughty cat was going to kill all the crickets. She picked up the cricket cage. She was thankful that it wasn't broken. The lid was okay as well.

Jenny looked up when someone opened the classroom door. Oh, no, it was Mrs. Perry. This was a terrible time for the principal to stop by. Mrs. Steele and Mrs. Perry watched as crickets jumped and kids ran after them. They both looked very serious.

Richard caught a cricket in his cupped hands.

Jenny held the cage out. Richard dumped one cricket inside, and Jenny held the lid in place. Kevin came toward her with cupped hands. She opened the lid partway and another cricket was back in captivity. Kids were still stooping and trying to catch runaway crickets. Munchkin sat with a slightly mangled cricket between his paws. He poked at the insect and it moved one leg.

Mrs. Perry whispered something to their teacher and left the room. Jenny was sure it had something to do with her bad cat. She walked to the front of the room and held out the cricket cage to Mrs. Steele. They had captured five crickets. Jenny watched her teacher's face, but couldn't tell if she was angry.

"Thank you, Jenny." Mrs. Steele took the cage and placed the crickets on the tall filing cabinet near her desk.

Maybe the crickets would be safe there. And maybe Mrs. Perry would let Munchkin stay in school if he didn't get into any more trouble.

Mrs. Steele announced that they were going to share the articles they wrote the day before.

Jenny looked down at her desk when Mrs. Steele called for volunteers. Her article still only had two sentences.

Kevin read his article. He had written about Rana. "Rana was born in Colorado. She has a little sister named Tara. She has a cat named Tiger. Rana's grandparents live in India. Rana has gone to India to visit them. I don't think it's fair that some kids get to travel far away. I've never been anywhere except Colorado and Kansas."

"Good, Kevin," said Mrs. Steele.

Susan raised her hand. "Kevin should have left out his own opinions."

"That's right," said Mrs. Steele. "Opinions should be in an editorial."

Kevin sneered at Susan when he walked past her.

Jenny didn't blame him. Sometimes Susan could be so annoying.

Richard shared his article next. "This is an editorial written by Munchkin." He cleared his throat.

Jenny wondered if he'd read it in his pretend cat voice.

Sure enough, he did. In his pretend cat voice Richard read, "I love school. I can't wait for the pet party. I hope lots of guinea pigs and hamsters and small birds and lizards come to our classroom. I'd love to trade valentines with them. School is so much better than living with that dope, Richard."

Everyone laughed. Even Mrs. Steele. But Jenny worried that their teacher wouldn't think it was funny if Munchkin kept getting into mischief.

"Okay," said their teacher. "We'll talk more about writing editorials next week."

That afternoon, Mrs. Steele told Jenny that Nando, the librarian, would be taking the cat home for the weekend.

Jenny tried to swallow the lump in her throat. She thought her teacher would take the cat home. Maybe her teacher didn't want to take a naughty, cricket-stealing cat home with her. "Munchkin doesn't know Nando," she finally said.

"That's why I think it would be a good idea for

you to take your cat to the library to meet him," said Mrs. Steele.

"Right now?" said Jenny.

"Yes," said her teacher. "You can read in the library while the rest of the class does silent reading in the classroom."

Jenny fished her book out of her desk and carried it to the front of the room. Munchkin was sleeping on their teacher's rocking chair again. Jenny put down her book and picked up the limp, sleepy cat. Munchkin lifted his head, glanced at Jenny, then nestled against her.

"Richard, could you help Jenny?" said Mrs. Steele, handing Jenny's book to him. "Open the library door for her, then come back and get the cat's litter box and food."

"Do I have to take the big bag of food?" Richard made his sad clown face.

"No, I've filled a plastic bag with enough food for the weekend," said Mrs. Steele.

Richard clicked his heels together when he opened the door to the library and motioned Jenny inside. "After you, madam."

Jenny wrinkled her nose at him.

"Ah yes, you, too, Mister Cat." Richard set the book on a table, saluted, and marched out.

Nando came out of his office. He had a ponytail and often told jokes. All the kids loved him. Jenny wondered if her cat would love him, too.

"So this is the famous cat," Nando said.

"This is Munchkin," said Jenny uncertainly. She wasn't sure why Nando thought her cat was famous.

Nando rubbed the cat's ears.

Munchkin started to purr.

"He really likes you." Jenny was surprised. Her cat usually didn't purr for a stranger.

Richard returned to the library with the litter box, the cat carrier, and a plastic bag full of other supplies.

"Put everything behind the library desk." Nando pointed out a spot, then turned back to Jenny. "I understand that your cat likes to chase crickets," he said with a grin.

"How did you hear about that?" Jenny asked.

"Several teachers were talking about it in the teachers' lounge at lunchtime," Nando told her.

Jenny was stunned. Now all the teachers would know that her cat was a problem.

A third-grade class began to file into the library.

"Take a seat, amigos," Nando told them, "and I'll be with you in a minute."

Several students gathered to pat the cat.

"Okay, Munchkin, it's story time." Nando put the cat down on the floor. "Make yourself at home."

The cat followed the students to the raised sitting area and sat next to a girl in the first row.

Jenny wondered if Munchkin thought he was a student now.

Nando began to read the first chapter from *Sarah, Plain and Tall*.

Munchkin stood up and strolled over to Nando.

The kids laughed.

"Would you like to sit with me?" Nando asked the cat.

Munchkin jumped into his lap.

"I think Munchkin knows that there's a cat in this book," said Nando.

Munchkin put his paw on the book.

"Do you want me to read more?" Nando asked the cat.

Munchkin sat down on Nando's lap and stared up at him.

"I guess that means yes." Nando continued to read the first chapter.

After the librarian finished the chapter, one of the boys said, "I want to read the book the cat likes."

"I have two copies of this book." Nando closed the book and held it up.

"I'll take the other one," said a girl in the front row who was missing a front tooth.

Nando stood up. "Follow me to the library desk." He carried Munchkin and the book to the checkout area, found the other copy, and handed the books to the two students.

Another student raced up to the desk. "I want a book about a cat, too," he said, "but the cat has to touch it first."

Nando smiled. "I think that can be arranged." Still holding the cat, he walked to the fiction shelves and pulled out another cat book.

Jenny noticed that Nando's black wool pants had little gray hairs all over them. Maybe she should tell him to wear gray pants if he wanted to hold her cat.

Nando set the book on one of the library tables. Munchkin sniffed the book, then sat down on it.

"Hey! He's sitting on it," said the boy.

Jenny picked the cat up, and the boy grabbed the book.

"Munchkin warmed it for you," Nando said, then winked at Jenny. "I think cat books are going to be very popular with Munchkin around."

Chapter 9

On Saturday morning Susan called.

Jenny was surprised. Susan didn't usually call her on a weekend.

Susan invited Jenny to go with her to Mary's house. They were going to work on costumes for the pet party. Valentine's Day was the following Thursday. Susan's mother drove both girls to Mary's house.

"Mary's mother sews clothes and place mats and even Halloween costumes," Susan explained. "So she has lots of fabric and thread and ribbon. We can make costumes for our cats and Mary's dog today. Then if we have time, we can make some things for other students who can't sew."

Jenny thought it would be a miracle if she made even one costume.

Mary's mother had a large sewing room with

two sewing machines. She had shelves stacked with fabric and plastic boxes full of silky ribbons of all colors, wide plaid ribbons, and even ribbons with sequins sewn on them.

Mary entered the room carrying another plastic box. "Here are some costumes my mother made when my brother and I were younger." She set the box on a big table and pulled out a blue cowboy vest with a matching felt hat. "This would probably fit my dog, Winston."

"The vest might fit," said Susan, "but the hat looks too big."

"We can make the hat smaller with a large safety pin." Mary's mother demonstrated by pinning the back of the hat. "Go get Winston, and we can see what he thinks about being a cowdog."

Mary led her German shepherd into the room and tried to wrestle him into the vest. "Mom, I can only get one of his front paws through the armhole."

Jenny was surprised that Winston was so patient.

Mary's mother snipped a new opening that ran from the top of the armhole to the neckline of the vest. "This will make it easier to get the vest on a dog. I'll just sew on some Velcro to attach the pieces of the vest. Now for the hat . . ." She put the hat on the dog's head. "Tah-dah! Winston, you look like a cowboy!"

Jenny didn't think the dog looked at all like a cowboy, but she had to admit that the hat looked cute from the front. From the back the hat looked like stampeding cows had run over it.

"Here's my brother's old Superman costume." Mary pulled out a blue shirt with a big red *S* on it.

"Maybe Munchkin could be Supercat," said Jenny. "But that shirt looks much too big."

"Hmmm," said Mary's mother, "what we could do is put a red *S* on a blue bandanna. That would be easier to put on a cat than a shirt." She cut a square of blue fabric. "Now, Jenny, take some paper and make an *S* that's small enough to fit on this bandanna, then cut it out in red felt."

Jenny worked on her Supercat bandanna while Mary's mother helped Susan make a princess dress for Portia.

"I want Portia's dress to be red and silky." Susan fingered a bolt of shiny fabric.

"That's taffeta, which might be a bit stiff," said Mary's mother. "Here's some crushed velvet, which would be softer."

"That's lovely." Susan rubbed her hand against

the fabric. "I'd also like some kind of fancy trim around the neckline."

Mary's mother pulled a plastic box from the shelf and placed it on the table. "Take a look in here."

Susan looked through the ribbons and lace and finally held up a red ribbon with blue and white sequins on it. "What do you think about this?"

"That would be nice," said Mary, pawing through another box. She held up some lace that was wound on a plastic holder. "This white lace would be very elegant."

"I agree." Mary's mother took the lace and held it against the red velvet fabric. "The scalloped edge of the lace will work well around the neckline."

"Portia will love it!" Susan's eyes sparkled.

"Do you have the cat's measurements?" Mary's mother asked.

"Right here." Susan pulled out a sheet of paper from her backpack as well as some checkered fabric. "I also took an old piece of material and wrapped it around Portia like a dress, cutting it to just the right size," Susan explained. "Here are holes for her front feet."

Mary's mother took the bolt of red velvet and unrolled enough for the cat's dress. Then she placed the checkered fabric on top of the velvet.

"I'll use this as a guide to cut the good fabric." She picked up some scissors and began to cut the velvet fabric. "I'll allow some extra fabric so the dress won't be too tight."

Jenny watched as Mary's mother cut the velvet. Portia's dress was going to be very fancy.

While Susan worked on sewing lace around the neck of the dress, Mary's mother examined the blue bandanna.

"Is your cat about the same size as Portia?" she asked.

"No, Munchkin is longer and fatter." Jenny was getting really excited about the pet party now. Munchkin would make a great Supercat. If he'd wear his costume.

Chapter 10

On Monday morning Jenny hurried to the library. Nando was checking in books, and Munchkin sat beside him.

"Munchkin is a good library helper," said Nando.

"Was he okay at your house this weekend?" Jenny asked.

"He was the perfect companion. He sat next to me while I read a book on Saturday, then watched football with me on Sunday."

Jenny beamed. "I wish Munchkin could be the school cat, then I could see him all the time."

"I'd like that," said Nando.

Jenny's smile turned to a frown. "Mrs. Steele only got permission for him to stay a week or two. I'm worried that if he gets into any more trouble, Mrs. Perry won't want him at our school. How can we make sure Munchkin stays here longer?"

"We should figure out some reasons why our school needs a cat, and then we should let people know about them."

"What about valentines?" said Jenny. "We could ask all the kids to write valentines to Munchkin and say why they like a cat at school."

"That's a very good idea," said Nando.

"I could make a mailbox for Munchkin's valentine cards," said Jenny. "Would it be okay to put it on the library desk?"

"Yes!" said Nando. "And I'll tell students to write the cards."

Jenny leaned over so that she was nose to nose with her cat. "Maybe you'll get to stay here, and I can see you every day!"

Munchkin licked Jenny's nose.

"Can my cat stay in the library with you today?" Jenny thought that might keep her cat from getting into mischief.

"Sure," said Nando. "I have several classes coming to the library, so he can get to know lots of students."

Susan was talking to Mrs. Steele when Jenny entered the classroom.

"Mary and Jenny and I made costumes over the

weekend," Susan announced. "Can we show the costumes to the class?"

"We have a busy morning with a math lesson followed by art and PE," their teacher said. "This afternoon would be better."

"We thought it would be nice to have Munchkin model the costumes," said Mary.

Richard must have overheard because he guffawed.

Jenny didn't think it was funny. She was sure her cat would hate being a model. He might hiss and spit and scratch Susan, which she deserved. But then Mrs. Steele would have even more reasons not to like Munchkin.

After lunch Susan and Mary displayed the pet costumes on the front row of desks.

"Where's Munchkin?" asked Susan.

"Probably in the library," said Jenny. "I'll go get him." She hoped her cat was sleeping because then he might put up with wearing an outfit or two.

Jenny went into the library, but Munchkin wasn't there. "Have you seen my cat?" Jenny asked Nando.

"I took Munchkin next door to Ms. Rogers's classroom when Mrs. Quinn's class came to the library to do research. Mrs. Quinn is allergic to cats."

"Oh, no!" Jenny was horrified. "Does that mean that Munchkin will have to leave the school?"

"No, I don't think so," said Nando. "Mrs. Quinn doesn't allow the cat in her classroom, so she hasn't had any problems with her allergies."

Jenny hurried to the first-grade classroom next door. Ms. Rogers's students were cutting out pictures of rain-forest animals.

"Have you seen Munchkin?" Jenny asked the teacher.

Ms. Rogers laughed. "Your cat really liked our rain-forest exhibit. He sat by the pool and watched the fish, then he ran off with the frog."

Jenny was shocked. "He stole your frog?"

"It's just a stuffed frog, not a live one," said the teacher. "I bought the frog at a pet store, so I think it's actually a cat toy."

Jenny was relieved that Ms. Rogers didn't seem mad, but she wondered where Munchkin had gone with the frog. She went to the second-grade classroom next, but the classroom was empty. She worried that Susan and Mary would be getting impatient. But it was good that Munchkin was getting to know more students. She wanted everyone to send valentines to her cat. She heard kids laughing in the third-grade classroom, so she hurried in there. One of the students pointed to the front of the room. Munchkin was standing on the teacher's desk looking over the edge. Uh-oh. The teacher was kneeling on the floor scooping dirt back into a flowerpot. Jenny didn't even have to ask what had happened. She knew Munchkin had knocked the plant off the desk.

Mrs. Perry walked into the classroom. She looked down at the dirt on the floor, then up at the cat. "I'll call the custodian to clean up the mess." The principal had on her grumpy face as she walked out of the room.

Mrs. Grant stood up. "There we go, good as new," she said as she placed the plant back on her desk.

Jenny rushed over and grabbed Munchkin before he sent the plant on another trip to the floor. As she carried her cat down the hall she worried about the naughty things he had done. Would anybody send valentines to a cat that kept getting into trouble?

When Jenny returned to her classroom, Mrs. Steele said, "Okay, class, put away your books. It's time for the fashion show."

Mary followed Susan to the front of the room and gave Jenny a dirty look. "What took you so long?"

"Munchkin wasn't in the library," Jenny explained. "I had to search for him."

"Sit in the rocking chair with the cat," Susan said, "and I'll hand you the costumes to put on him."

Jenny sat down. Munchkin sat down on her lap.

"Here's the princess dress that my cat, Portia, will wear." Susan held the dress up before handing it to Jenny. "Look how the front opens completely to make putting it on easy."

Munchkin didn't seem bothered by the dress at first. Jenny fastened the Velcro and held the cat so that he was standing on her lap.

Susan ran over with a gold crown, which she set on Munchkin's head.

Munchkin swatted the crown off his head. Then he jumped to the ground and rolled around, trying to get rid of the dress.

"Way to go, Munchkin!" said Richard.

Everyone in the class laughed.

Jenny held the cat still while Susan unfastened the Velcro and removed the dress. Munchkin sat on the floor and licked his chest.

The Supercat costume was next. When Mary tried to put the bandanna around the cat's neck, he swatted her hand and tried to bite her.

"I think Munchkin's modeling career is over for the moment," said Mrs. Steele.

Jenny worried that his school career was over as well. Why would anyone want such a difficult cat at school? Especially when one of the teachers was allergic to him.

Chapter 11

On Tuesday, Jenny carried her decorated box to the library. She had covered the box with pink paper, then glued lots of hearts all over it. On one side she had glued a photograph of her cat. Above the picture she had written, "Valentines for Munchkin."

"That looks great!" Nando set the box on the front desk.

"Do you think Munchkin will get many valentines?" Jenny asked.

"I'm sure he will," said Nando.

"Have you seen my cat this morning?" asked Jenny.

Nando shook his head.

Jenny headed to the first-grade classroom first, but the cat wasn't there. She checked several more classrooms, but he wasn't in any of them. She was beginning to get scared that Munchkin was lost. Then a tall boy came around the corner carrying her cat.

"Oh, Munchkin, where have you been?" Jenny held out her arms toward the cat.

"Is this your cat?" The boy held out the cat. "He is so stubborn. He keeps trying to come into our classroom. We shut the door, but he waits until someone goes out and then he dashes inside."

Jenny took the cat and held him close. She was relieved to have him back but curious at the same time. "Why do you think he likes your classroom so much?"

The boy shrugged. "I don't know, but our teacher doesn't like cats. She's allergic to them."

"Is your teacher Mrs. Quinn?"

The boy nodded.

Jenny sighed. Her cat kept getting into trouble. He certainly wouldn't get any valentines from Mrs. Quinn or anyone in her class. It was bad enough that Mrs. Quinn was allergic, but Munchkin was being a real pest. Jenny took her cat to the library and left him sitting by his valentine box, looking angelic.

When Jenny entered her classroom, she saw that Mrs. Steele was wearing her flight attendant outfit. She had on a navy blue skirt and jacket with a white blouse, navy stockings, and shoes to match. Jenny imagined her handing out soda and pretzels.

Instead, her teacher was writing on the board. Jenny noticed that she'd gotten white chalk dust on her sleeve.

"Today we're going to write editorials," Mrs. Steele said. "In an editorial you want to state your opinion about something, like we talked about. But you also should present some facts about why you feel that way. Then you should draw a conclusion from the facts." She pointed to the board, where she had written, "*Opinion, Facts, Conclusion.*"

Jenny had an opinion about her cat. Her cat should stay with her at school forever. Now she just needed facts and the conclusion. If only her cat would do something to make everyone love him instead of being naughty all the time.

"Some people think you should go to school in the summer," said their teacher. "What do you think about that?"

"I wouldn't like it," said Kevin. "I need a vacation from this place."

Mrs. Steele nodded agreement. "That's one reason. Can you think of anything else?"

"It's too hot in the summer," said Richard, "and

I wouldn't have as much time to practice for the swim team."

"Those are more good reasons," said Mrs. Steele. "And if swim team is really important to you, you might say that in your conclusion. Now I want all of you to write an editorial."

Jenny decided to write about her cat. She wrote, "I think Munchkin should be the school cat. He needs a new home, and he likes it at school." She stopped writing. She couldn't think of anything else. Did she need more reasons? She glanced over at Susan, who was writing and writing. Susan probably had one hundred reasons already.

When Mrs. Steele asked for someone to read their editorial, Susan's hand shot up.

Susan read, "I think we should have a salad bar for school lunch. My mother packs a healthy lunch for me every day. She wouldn't have to do that if our school lunches weren't so disgusting. Salad is much healthier for you than greasy hamburgers. Vegetables and fruit are important in a healthy diet. Many children are overweight. They wouldn't weigh so much if they ate more vegetables. Therefore, I think our school cafeteria should have a salad bar."

"Very good, Susan." Mrs. Steele smiled at her. "Anyone else?"

Mary read her editorial. "I think having a class pet party is a good idea for Valentine's Day. Instead of eating too much candy, we get to see other people's pets. Making costumes is fun, too. I'm going to give my dog a bath the day before the party so he'll be very clean. That's why I think a pet party is a good idea."

Mrs. Steele laughed. "Very nice. And I can't wait to see your very clean dog on Valentine's Day."

Jenny hoped nobody expected her to wash her cat for the party.

It was time for recess. Jenny put on her coat, hat, and mittens, but before going outside, she went to the library to check on her cat. He wasn't there. She headed for Mrs. Quinn's room. Sure enough, she found Munchkin crouching in the hall near the door, just waiting for his chance to rush inside and surprise the teacher.

Jenny grabbed her cat. "No, no, no," she told him as she carried him swiftly down the hall. "You're going to get thrown out of school if you keep pestering Mrs. Quinn."

Chapter 12

Jenny shivered when she awoke the next morning. She pulled her quilt up so that it covered her nose and wished she could cuddle with a warm kitty. Her very own warm kitty.

When she finally got up, she pulled on her slippers, then looked out the window. Big white flakes of snow were falling. The pine trees had mounds of snow on every branch. No cars drove by her house. Everything was frosted and still.

Her mother poked her head into the room. "No school today," she said.

"Oh, no!" Normally Jenny loved snow days. But not today. "Munchkin will be all alone."

"I'm sure the kitty will be fine," said her mother.

Jenny wasn't sure at all. What if the heating was off and the cat was cold and frightened? What if the electricity was off, too? What if it snowed and snowed and there was no school on Valentine's Day? They wouldn't be able to have a pet party.

Jenny put on warm pants and a sweater, then hurried downstairs. "Can you drive me to school?" she asked her mother. "I want to see if Munchkin is okay."

"It will take a while to shovel the driveway." Her mother was stirring something in a bowl. "Besides, they're advising not to go out unless it's an emergency."

"This is an emergency!" said Jenny. "My cat is all alone at school."

"I know you're worried about Munchkin. Maybe you can walk over to school with a friend later, but I don't think anyone will be there to let you in."

"At least I can look in the window and wave to Munchkin." Jenny looked in the bowl.

"I'm making pancakes." Her mother leaned down and got a griddle out of a drawer. "Would you like some?"

"Sure." Jenny loved pancakes and syrup. Usually her mother made them only on weekends.

After Jenny had finished eating, she went outside to help her father clear the driveway and the sidewalk, but the snow was too deep and heavy for her.

"Do you think I could walk to school soon?" she asked her father.

"If you wait a few hours, then people will have had time to shovel their walks."

Hours! Jenny didn't want to wait for hours. She went inside and finished writing valentines for her classmates. She also made a big valentine to put inside Munchkin's valentine box. "A kitty is nice to have on a snowy day," she wrote. A kitty was nice to have anytime.

Finally she called Richard. "I want to be sure that Munchkin is okay. Will you walk to school with me?"

"Sure," said Richard. "I'll be right over."

Jenny put on her parka and watched for him through the front window.

Richard arrived with a bulging backpack. "I've got a thermos of hot chocolate and some cookies."

"Maybe I should get a snack for the kitty, too. In case he's run out of food." Jenny searched the refrigerator. She found the remains of a barbecued chicken and sawed off a few chunks for the cat.

Richard helped himself to one of the chunks. "Walking in the snow takes extra energy," he said, grinning.

Jenny didn't feel like eating cold chicken. Richard ate two leftover pancakes before they set off into the snow. Some people had shoveled their walks, but lots of people hadn't. Richard went first in his big blue boots. Jenny tried to step in the holes he'd made, but sometimes they were too far apart. "Take smaller steps," she said.

Richard took tiny, mincing steps. "Like this," he twittered.

"You were taking giant steps before," Jenny told him.

When they reached the school, the parking lot was empty. They walked around to their classroom window and peered inside. Jenny couldn't see her cat. "Where do you think Munchkin is?"

"He probably found a warm spot to sleep," said Richard.

"He's not on Mrs. Steele's rocking chair," said Jenny. "What's that scratchy noise?"

"Maybe it's your cat trying to claw his way into the cafeteria," said Richard.

Jenny glared at him.

"Or it could be someone shoveling their sidewalk."

They followed the scratching sound and discovered John, the custodian, shoveling the walk in front of the school. He grinned at them. "No school today, kids."

"Is my cat okay?" Jenny asked. "You know, the cat that lives in Mrs. Steele's room."

"He's fine," said John. "In fact, he caught two mice last night."

"Did he eat them?" Richard asked.

"No, the cat stood next to the mice and seemed very proud of himself," said John. "I told him he's a good boy and gave him some cat food. I often feed him when I arrive in the morning."

"Did he catch the mice in our classroom?" Jenny asked.

"No," said John. "It wasn't your classroom. Sometimes the cat follows me around while I inspect each classroom for problems like leaks or broken windows. He was real interested in one particular room, sniffing all around it, so I let him spend the night there."

"What if we have a really big blizzard?" asked Jenny. "Will you still be able to get to school?"

"I live two blocks away, and I have a jeep with a snowplow on front," said John. "I can always get to the school."

"We couldn't see Munchkin anywhere when we looked in the window," said Richard.

"I moved him to the library earlier because I suspect there might be mice in there."

"Mice that read books?" asked Jenny.

"Mice that nibble on books and other things, like candy and chewing gum in teachers' desks," said the custodian. "Would you like to visit Munchkin for a few minutes?" He unlocked the door and led them inside. "Leave your boots here so I don't have to clean the floors again."

Jenny thought it was fun to walk through the

empty school in her stocking feet. The hallways were very quiet.

Munchkin was sleeping on the couch in the library. He looked up when Jenny patted him and purred after she gave him some chicken.

"Do you think we'll have school tomorrow?" Jenny asked after they left the library and walked back to the front door.

"The snow has stopped," John said. "I'll have the walks and parking lot cleaned off soon."

"Good," said Jenny.

"Good?" said Richard.

"Tomorrow's the pet party," said Jenny. "You wouldn't want to miss that!"

Richard smiled. "You're right. It might be really exciting. Maybe the pets will get into a big fight and try to eat one another."

"That won't happen!" At least, Jenny hoped it wouldn't.

Chapter 13

School was open the next day. Jenny was excited because it was Valentine's Day. In her backpack, Jenny carried all the valentines she'd written, as well as the Supercat costume.

When she entered the classroom, she looked for her cat, but he wasn't there. She was about to search for him when Munchkin ran into the room carrying something in his mouth.

"Ohhhh, it's a mouse!" said Susan.

Munchkin laid the mouse at Jenny's feet.

"What a nice gift!" said Richard.

Jenny stared at the small brown creature. It lay on its side and didn't move. She didn't think a dead mouse was a nice gift.

Munchkin grabbed the lifeless rodent and ran out of the room with it.

"Your cat thinks you didn't appreciate your present," said Richard.

Jenny ignored him and hurried after her cat. She could hear students in the hallway yelling, "Look at that cat. What's he got in his mouth?"

John, the custodian, came around the corner, and Munchkin stopped beside him, setting the mouse down. "What a good kitty!" he said as he picked up the mouse.

Munchkin rubbed against John's leg.

"This is the third mouse he's caught this week," John told Jenny.

"Is the mousie dead or just sleeping?" asked a little boy.

"I think he might be sleeping," said the custodian. "I'll take him with me and let him finish his nap."

Jenny smiled at John. She liked what he told the little kid about the mouse, even if it wasn't the truth. She knelt down and patted Munchkin. She was glad he'd done something good for once. Then she gathered the cat into her arms and carried him to the library. Because of all the pets coming in and out of Jenny's classroom that afternoon, her cat had to spend the day in the library. Mrs. Steele had sent a schedule home with each student. The dogs could come at one o'clock and stay for half an hour. The small pets in cages, like hamsters or lizards, could come at one thirty. And the cats could come one at a time at two o'clock, after all the other pets had left. There were three cats coming to the party, and each one had his own special five minutes to be in the classroom. Munchkin was going to be the last cat to come into the room and show off his costume. At least, Jenny hoped her cat would wear his costume. She was never sure what her cat would do.

After lunch Jenny went to the library with the bandanna. Munchkin was sitting on Nando's lap.

Jenny held out the bandanna with the big red *S* on it. "You're going to look so handsome in your costume," she told the cat.

The cat stared at her like he didn't know what she was talking about.

"Would you keep the costume in your office?" Jenny asked. "I'll come over and dress him right before his time at the party."

"Sure," said Nando.

Jenny went over and shook the valentine box. There were some cards inside. She couldn't tell how many.

"Please be a good cat today," Jenny told Munchkin before returning to the classroom.

Mrs. Steele was still pouring punch into a glass bowl when the first dog arrived with Mary's mother. It was Winston, the cowdog, already wearing his vest and hat. Mary went over to her dog and hugged him.

Susan was taking notes and speaking into a small tape recorder. "Winston, our first party guest, is wearing a handsome blue vest with a matching hat. Winston belongs to Mary."

"Your dog looks great!" said their teacher, hurrying to her desk to grab her camera.

"Can we take his leash off for a minute?" Mary knelt by her pet. "A cowdog wouldn't wear one."

Mary's mother took off his leash and stepped away while Mrs. Steele took the picture.

Richard's mother was pulled into the room by Wolf. Winston stood up and started toward Richard's dog, but Mary's mother said, "Sit," and Winston sat down immediately.

Jenny was impressed. If she told Munchkin to sit, he'd probably spring into the air and land on a table.

Wolf was wearing a red bandanna. Richard's

mother wore a red cowboy hat. "Wolf wouldn't wear the hat," she explained.

Susan spoke into the recorder again. "Wolf, who belongs to Richard, is wearing a handsome red bandanna."

"Come on up and get your picture taken, Richard," said Mrs. Steele.

"Wait a second while I get my cowboy boots on." Richard went to his cubby and clomped back down the aisle wearing his blue rubber boots.

"Would you like to wear the hat?" Richard's mother removed her hat and offered it to Richard.

"Go ahead," Mrs. Steele encouraged. "It will make a great picture."

Richard put on the hat, pulling it low over his eyes, then sat next to his dog. Wolf wagged his tail.

"I can't see your face," said their teacher.

"That's the idea," said Richard.

Several more dogs arrived. Samantha, the Scottie dog, wore a pink coat, which Susan said was lovely against the dog's black fur. Another Chihuahua wore pearls and a pink party hat. Mrs. Steele had dog treats for all of them.

Kids drank punch and ate heart-shaped cookies with red sprinkles on them and walked around patting the dogs. Richard slipped a cookie to Wolf.

"It's almost time for all the dogs to leave," announced Mrs. Steele. "Have I taken pictures of all the dogs and the students who belong to them?"

"My mother couldn't come today with my dog," said Eliseo. "Could I have my picture taken with your dog, Richard?"

"Sure," said Richard. "And you can even wear the hat."

Eliseo knelt beside Wolf and looked happy to wear the cowboy hat.

Kristen's mother came in carrying a hamster in a clear plastic ball. "I can't stay," she explained as she handed the ball to her daughter. "I have to pick your brother up at preschool, but I'll be back when school's over."

Mrs. Steele put her hand on Kristen's shoulder. "Your hamster looks so cute. But don't put him on the floor yet." She nodded at the dogs.

As soon as the last dog left, Susan announced, "Our first small animal is Furry, the hamster, wearing the cutest little red tutu."

Kristen put her hamster on the floor, and it ran and ran inside the ball, which made the ball roll around the classroom.

"Calling all cats!" Richard said in a low voice. "Rodent in a tutu, wrapped up like a present."

Jenny shot him a dirty look.

Kevin's father entered the classroom carrying a yellow snake in an aquarium that had red and green bows stuck to it. The snake was coiled up in one corner. It had one red ribbon tied around its body as well.

Susan announced, "Ratty, Kevin's snake, is in his fancy glass house, which has been decorated with colorful bows."

After that, there was a turtle with a bow stuck on his shell and a lizard with a ribbon around his neck. Susan announced that Gertie, the guinea pig, was Superpig. Everyone laughed as the guinea pig waddled around the room wearing a tiny red cape.

Finally it was time for the cats to take center stage. Susan's mother arrived with Portia in a pet carrier that had lacy red hearts stuck to it. Susan opened the carrier door, and Portia stepped out.

"Portia, a cat with a nose for fashion, is wearing a red velvet gown with white lace at the neck," Susan announced. "Notice the white hearts embroidered around the neck and hem of the gown." Portia walked regally to Susan's mother, who picked her up and smiled proudly.

Jenny noticed that the bottom of the cat's fancy

schmancy dress dragged on the ground. No wonder the cat had to walk slowly and carefully.

"I hope Munchkin will wear his costume today," Jenny whispered to Richard.

"Don't worry," Richard whispered back. "If he won't wear the costume, I have the perfect announcement."

"What?" Jenny raised her eyebrows.

"Munchkin, a cat with a nose for fashion, is wearing a gray fur coat with white trim at the neck." Richard said it softly and pretended to speak into a microphone.

Still, Susan must have known he was making fun of her because she glared at him.

Jenny couldn't help laughing. As usual, Richard's jokes made her feel better.

After Mrs. Steele had taken several pictures of Susan and her cat, Rana's mother came into the room. She was carrying a plain gray cat crate.

Susan kissed her cat before putting her back into the heart-decorated carrier.

Once Susan's mother left, Rana opened the door to the crate, but Tiger wouldn't come out. When Rana reached in, the cat crouched in the back of the crate and hissed.

"Please come out, Tiger," said Rana.

"You could shake her out," suggested Kevin.

"That would be mean," said Rana. "Tiger is scared."

"I'll tell everyone what Tiger is wearing," said Susan, kneeling down and looking through the crate door. Tiger hissed at her, too. Susan turned on her tape recorder and talked into it. "Tiger, Rana's tabby cat, is wearing a red knitted vest with some writing on it. What does it say?"

"It says 'Have a Beary Merry Christmas,'" said Rana. "The vest belongs to one of my stuffed bears."

Susan continued to talk into the tape recorder. "The vest has 'Merry Christmas' written on the front. Tiger obviously likes Christmas better than Valentine's Day."

Mrs. Steele took a photograph of Rana holding the cat's crate, since Tiger still refused to come out.

Finally it was Munchkin's turn to make his modeling debut. Jenny hurried into the library. Would her cat act like a supercat?

Nando led Jenny to the cat's favorite bench, where Munchkin was sound asleep.

Jenny tied the bandanna around her cat's neck. The cat opened one eye but shut it again.

Jenny picked up the sleepy cat and carried him into the classroom.

"Here is Munchkin," Susan announced, "wearing a deep blue bandanna with a bold red *S* on it. Welcome to the party, Supercat."

Jenny was pleased. Susan had made a nice announcement about her cat. And Munchkin was being ever so good. He sat quietly on Jenny's lap while Mrs. Steele took his picture.

But then he looked around and spotted the tutu-clad hamster. Suddenly alert, he stood up on Jenny's lap ready to launch an attack. She tried to hold on to him, but he dug his claws into her leg and sprang to the floor.

Munchkin shot across the room, his bandanna flying like a cape. He stood on his hind legs, one paw on Kristen's chair. With the other paw he batted at the hamster's ball.

Kristen screamed and held her hamster in the air.

"Somebody get that cat!" Susan yelled.

But Munchkin leaped onto the desk next to Kristen and reached for the hamster again.

Kristen stood up, clutching the plastic ball to her chest.

Jenny rushed over and grabbed up her cat. Why couldn't her cat be good like Susan's cat? Why did he always get into trouble?

As Jenny carried Munchkin back to the library she worried that no one would want her cat at school. He wasn't a supercat. He was a superbad cat.

Chapter 14

Nando came out of his office. "You don't look very happy. Wasn't Supercat a hit?"

"Not really," said Jenny. "He tried to eat the hamster."

"Well, cats are hunters. They're supposed to catch rodents."

"I'm afraid he's too naughty to be a school cat," said Jenny.

"I'm not so sure about that. I think we should look at Munchkin's valentines." Nando carried the heart-decorated box to a table. "Kids have been bringing them in all afternoon."

"Really?" Jenny put her cat down and picked up the box. It was heavy. She opened the box and turned it over. Envelopes and red hearts and folded papers spilled all over the table.

Jenny could hardly believe it. Maybe there was

hope after all. She sat down by the table, pulled Munchkin onto her lap, and showed him a red envelope. "Look! This is for you." The cat sniffed the card.

Richard came into the library. "Hey, are all these valentines for the cat?" Richard picked one up and read it. " 'You are more important than ever now because there are mice in our school. P.S. I am not afraid of mice. Harrison.' "

They all laughed.

Jenny had already written about mice in her editorial. She needed a different reason why a school cat was important. She picked up a card and read aloud. " 'Dear Munchkin, I think you are silly when you leap into Mrs. Steele's chair. It is so funny when you sleep there. Love, Rana.' "

"Oh, this one is nice." Richard read, " 'Dear Munchkin, I like you because when I am sad, you cheer me up. From Liam.' "

"That is nice," said Jenny. "Who's Liam?"

"He's in third grade," said Nando. "His class was in the library on Monday."

Munchkin jumped onto the table and sniffed the mountain of cards, then sat down on some of them.

"See," said Nando, "Munchkin likes getting

valentines." He picked up a sheet of paper with hearts at the top. " 'We have a school cat named Munchkin. He is very funny. One time he went into the girls' bathroom and he's a boy. I love cats. Sincerely, Joey.' "

Richard and Nando laughed.

Jenny had to smile. Life was never dull with Munchkin around.

"This kid wrote a poem." Richard held up a red heart with writing inside it. He read, " 'Roses are red, violets are blue, you are a cat friend, and I like you.' "

"That's sweet!" Jenny agreed.

"These are great." Nando had several cards in his hand. "Listen to this one: 'Dear Munchkin, I appreciate you because not many schools have their own school cat. Everyone loves you! You also get into lots of mischief. Remember the time you got into my lunch bag and tried to eat my sandwich? From Emma.' "

"Maybe kids love the mischief," said Jenny, "but what about the teachers?"

"Oh, I think a lot of teachers appreciate your cat." Nando picked up another card and read it. "This card says it all: 'Dear Munchkin, I love how you make us laugh.' "

"I think that's the most important thing about Munchkin," said Richard. "He makes people laugh."

Nando nodded. "I agree. School can get stressful for kids. It's good to take a break and laugh once in a while."

"Should I put that in my editorial?" Jenny asked.

"Definitely," said Nando.

"And you should also tell how many valentines Munchkin got," said Richard. "I think it's a school record. Even I didn't get this many valentines."

While Richard counted valentines and Nando took off the cat's costume, Jenny finished her editorial.

I think we need a school cat. We have mice running around at night eating chewing gum and candy and books. There are other reasons, too. School is stressful for kids. Sometimes kids are sad. Munchkin got one hundred and three valentines. Students wrote why they like him. They like the mischief that he gets into because it makes them laugh. And when they laugh, they don't feel sad or stressed anymore. That's why our school needs Munchkin.

Chapter 15

Munchkin greeted Jenny as soon as she came in the classroom the next day. She leaned over and picked her cat up. He put his paw on her cold face. She loved being able to see him every day. But how much longer would he be able to stay at school?

Jenny squinted at the large wall calendar. Munchkin's first day in the classroom had been on Thursday, the week before. Today was Friday, the end of the cat's second week in the classroom. And Mrs. Steele had said he could stay for a week or two. Did she mean two whole weeks? But then Mrs. Perry said the cat could stay if he didn't cause trouble, and he'd caused a lot of trouble. The principal also said he couldn't bother anyone with allergies. But he had bothered Mrs. Quinn a lot. Jenny worried that if her editorial didn't work,

Munchkin would have to leave school soon. Maybe by next Wednesday, or even earlier.

Jenny knelt down by her cubby, setting the cat on the floor. He scampered away. She took off her coat and hung it up. As she approached her desk she could see her cat playing with something underneath it. "Oh, Munchkin, did you steal the frog again?"

The cat leaped onto her desk with the toy frog in his mouth, then stretched out on her desk with the stolen toy between his front paws.

Jenny didn't know whether to laugh or cry. She hoped the third-grade teacher still thought her cat was funny.

"Today we're going to put our class newspaper together," said Mrs. Steele. "There are a few things we need to figure out first." She drew a rectangle on the board. "This is the front page. We need a name for our newspaper. We could call it *Fourth-grade Features* or *The Classroom Communicator* or something like that. Any ideas?"

"We could call it *The Classroom Channel*," said Susan.

"How about *Classroom Chatter*?" said Mary.

Jenny didn't really care what they called the

newspaper. She looked down at her kitty's face—his pink nose, his long white whiskers, the fur inside his ears. He licked her hand with his sandpaper tongue.

"What about *Fourth-grade Faces?*" said Rana.

"If we called it *Fourth-grade Faces,* we could put a picture of each student with his or her article," suggested Richard.

"That's a great idea," said Mrs. Steele.

They took a vote on the names, and almost everyone liked Rana's name.

Their teacher wrote *"Fourth-Grade Faces"* on the board. "The front page of the paper will have several articles on it as well as pictures. The banner headline describes the most important article on the front page. Can someone give me an example of a headline for an article?"

Susan's hand shot up. "Pet Party a Big Success," she said.

"Good." Mrs. Steele wrote Susan's headline on the front page. "A headline is a short sentence that describes the article." She smiled at Susan. "And the pet party was lots of fun."

Jenny rolled her eyes. No matter what happened, Susan's article would be on the front page. And Jenny's article would be on the last page.

"I want each of you to select your best article and write a headline for it," said Mrs. Steele. "Then put your article on my desk. I'll read your articles and edit them. Susan and Mary will help me."

Jenny took her article out of her desk. She didn't know what to write for her headline. She also didn't have any place to write, since her cat was on her desk. She pulled him onto her lap and put her article on top of her desk. He jumped back onto her desk and lay down on her article. She pulled him into her lap again, but now there were cat hairs on her paper. Maybe they'd be good luck.

She wrote, "SCHOOL CAT EDITORIAL," at the top of the page and put her editorial on Mrs. Steele's desk. She hoped Mrs. Steele would like what she'd written. More than that, she hoped it would convince her teacher that Munchkin had an important job at school and needed to stay.

Susan and Mary skipped morning and lunch recess because they were working with Mrs. Steele on all the articles. They even skipped music class.

When the class returned to the room after music, Mrs. Steele sat down in her rocking chair and said, "Come up front and sit down. I want to show you our progress so far on our newspaper." She had several pieces of paper in her lap.

Jenny wondered if Mrs. Steele had read her editorial yet. She'd called several kids to the front of the room to make changes to their articles. Maybe her article was so bad, it couldn't be fixed. Munchkin sat down beside Jenny, which made her feel better.

Once everyone sat down, Mrs. Steele said, "You all had really good articles. At first we decided to put Susan's article at the top of the first page, since she wrote about our big event this week, which seemed like the most important news item." She held up a sheet of paper.

Jenny could read the big headline: PET PARTY A SUCCESS. Susan's picture was next to a long article that took up a lot of the page. No surprise there.

"I really liked Richard's suggestion about having a picture of each student by his or her article. We have good pictures of everyone at the pet party. So that also made it important to have Susan's article on the first page."

And Susan's such a good writer and does everything perfectly, thought Jenny.

"But then we had another article, which I showed to the principal." Mrs. Steele looked at

Jenny and smiled. "Jenny has been working on an editorial about why Munchkin should be our official school cat."

Jenny held her breath. Had her editorial worked? She placed her hand on Munchkin's back. He crossed his paws and stared up at her.

"So we changed the front page," Mrs. Steele continued, "because now we have some late-breaking news."

Jenny was confused. Late-breaking news? Was that hard news or soft news? Good news or bad news?

"Jenny, why don't you come up front and read our new banner headline and article to the class?" Mrs. Steele smiled again.

Jenny noticed that Susan was smiling, too. She took the new page from her teacher with shaking hands. She read the headline slowly to herself: "Munchkin Earns School Cat Position." It was almost too good to be true. Jenny looked at her teacher with her mouth open.

Mrs. Steele smiled encouragement. "Go ahead. Read it to the class."

Jenny took a deep breath. "After reading a student editorial, Mrs. Perry agreed that the school

needs a school cat who makes everyone laugh. She said she was worried at first because a teacher with allergies was against having a cat at school. But after Munchkin caught two mice in her classroom, the teacher changed her mind. The principal said, 'Munchkin has my permission to stay at our school as long as he likes.' "

Jenny beamed. She was so happy, she was afraid

she'd cry. Munchkin must have known something important had happened because he trotted over and nudged her ankle. She picked him up, buried her face in his soft fur, and he purred and purred and purred.

Ann Whitehead Nagda is the author of the popular chapter books that are companions to *The Valentine Cat*: *Dear Whiskers, Meow Means Mischief, Tarantula Power!*, and *The Perfect Cat-Sitter*, as well as several award-winning math titles for children. Munchkin is based on her own cat, Tigger, and on a school cat named Sooty in Portland, Oregon. She followed Sooty around for a day and observed him visiting classrooms and interacting with students, which gave her lots of ideas for this book. She lives in Colorado.

Stephanie Roth has illustrated many chapter books for young readers, including all of the books about Jenny and her friends, as well as the books in Colleen O'Shaughnessy McKenna's Third Grade series. She has also illustrated full color picture books. Of *Two Christmas Mice* by Corinne Demas, *Booklist* noted her "delightfully expressive" art. She lives on the California coast.